Barbie™

The Nutcracker

By Sue Kassirer
Photographed by Jeff O'Brien, Laura Lynch,
Tim Geisen, Darin Pappas, Steve Toth, Lisa Collins, and Judy Tsuno
Illustrated by S.I. Artists

🌸 A GOLDEN BOOK • NEW YORK

BARBIE and associated trademarks and trade dress are owned by, and used under license from, Mattel.
©2002, 2021 Mattel.
www.barbie.com

Published in the United States by Golden Books, an imprint of Random House Children's Books, a division of Penguin Random House LLC, 1745 Broadway, New York, NY 10019, and in Canada by Penguin Random House Canada Limited, Toronto. Originally published in slightly different form in the United States by Golden Books, an imprint of Random House Children's Books, a division of Penguin Random House LLC, New York, in 2002. Golden Books, A Golden Book, A Little Golden Book, the G colophon, and the distinctive gold spine are registered trademarks of Penguin Random House LLC.
rhcbooks.com
ISBN 978-0-307-99512-4 (trade)
Printed in the United States of America
10 9 8 7 6 5 4 3 2 1
2021 Golden Books Edition

A hush falls over the audience as the musicians begin to play. The curtain rises. The Nutcracker Ballet is about to begin!

Onstage, at a festive Christmas party, a girl named Clara is given a gift from her uncle. It is a beautiful nutcracker, shaped like a soldier.

Clara loves her nutcracker. She holds him tight as she dances around the room.

That night, after the Christmas party, Clara cannot sleep. She keeps thinking about her nutcracker and tiptoes downstairs to find him.

Hugging her dear nutcracker close,
Clara falls sound asleep on the sofa.

Suddenly, Clara opens her eyes . . . and gasps!
For the toys are alive—and as tall as Clara!

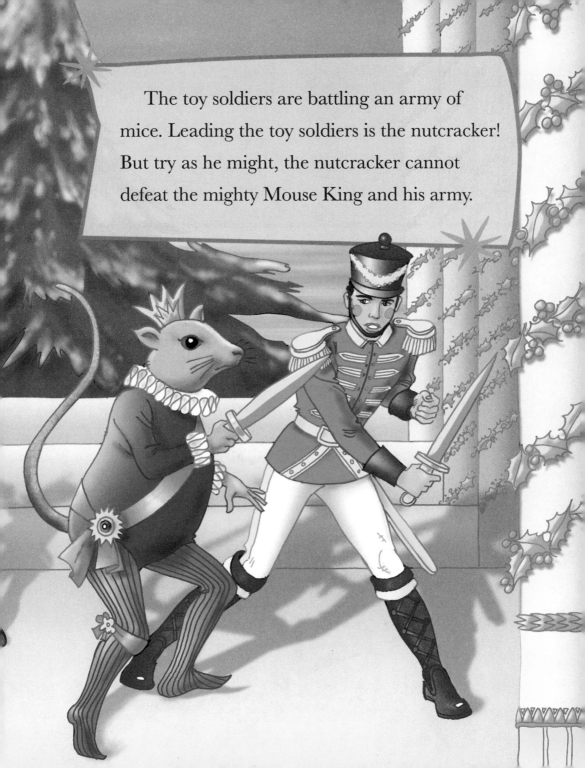

The toy soldiers are battling an army of mice. Leading the toy soldiers is the nutcracker! But try as he might, the nutcracker cannot defeat the mighty Mouse King and his army.

Quietly, Clara comes up from behind the Mouse King and pulls his tail. With a shrill cry, the Mouse King and his troops scurry away. And the nutcracker turns into a handsome prince!

"You have saved my life," the prince says to Clara. "To thank you, let me take you to my home, the Kingdom of Sweets!"

The prince leads Clara outside, through the magical Christmas Woods.

When Clara and the prince arrive at the palace, the Sugar Plum Fairy seats them on a golden throne for two. It's time for a festival in their honor to begin!

There is a dance of peppermint candy . . .

and hot chocolate . . .

. . . and tea!

Even the flowers waltz in the Kingdom of Sweets.

Best of all, the Sugar Plum Fairy dances with her soldier.

Clara longs to stay in the Kingdom of Sweets forever! But now the festival is over, and it's time to fly home in the prince's royal sleigh.

As the beautiful sleigh rises into the air, Clara waves good-bye to the dancers and the Kingdom of Sweets.

"Good-bye, Clara! Good-bye!" call the dancers.

Clara opens her eyes and yawns. It's Christmas morning!

In Clara's arms is her dear nutcracker. And in her heart forever is the memory of the Kingdom of Sweets and her kind and handsome prince.